Little One

JO WEAVER

Hodder
Children's
Books

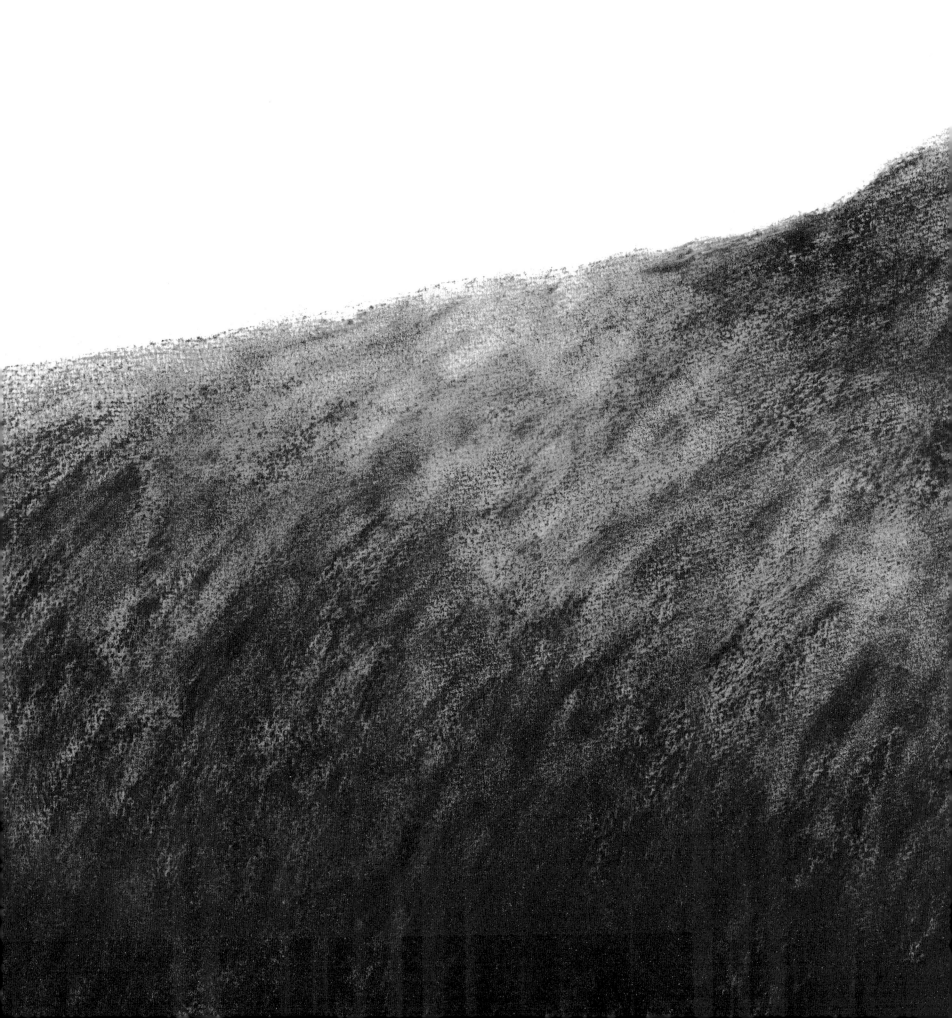

Big Bear stepped out of her winter den.

By her side, half asleep and blinking in the spring sunshine,

wobbled a tiny cub.

'There's so much to discover in your new world, Little One,'

said Big Bear.

She led her cub to the forest where new life was stirring

among the trees.

'This is where our journey begins,' she said.

Big Bear showed Little One how to be gentle with friends...

...and how to play all through the long summer days.

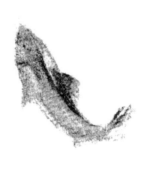

Little One watched Big Bear and learned how to fish…

…and how to swim safely in the cool forest lake.

'I'm with you, Little One,' said Big Bear.

Together they explored far and wide...

...and filled their hungry tummies

with ripe autumn berries.

Little One played in the blustery wind.

But Big Bear felt restless...

She knew that winter was coming.

It began to snow and as cold flakes settled on the ground,

Big Bear led their way out of the forest.

Together they

climbed up the hillside.

For a moment, they stopped

to look back at their land,

now covered in snow.

The wind roared and the snow piled high,

but Big Bear found their old den...

…and it smelled of home.

In the warm darkness, Big Bear and Little One

curled up together and waited for spring.

For Mum and Dad,
who read to me then.
And for Dom,
who reads to me now.

First published in 2016 by Hodder Children's Books
© Jo Weaver 2016

Hodder Children's Books
An imprint of Hachette Children's Group
Part of Hodder & Stoughton
Carmelite House
50 Victoria Embankment
London EC4Y 0DZ

ISBN: 978 1 444 92273 8

An Hachette UK Company
www.hachette.co.uk